WELCOME TO
PASSPORT TO READING
A beginning reader's ticket to a brand-new world!

Every book in this program is designed to build read-along and read-alone skills, level by level, through engaging and enriching stories. As the reader turns each page, he or she will become more confident with new vocabulary, sight words, and comprehension.

These PASSPORT TO READING levels will help you choose the perfect book for every reader.

READING TOGETHER
Read short words in simple sentence structures together to begin a reader's journey.

READING OUT LOUD
Encourage developing readers to sound out words in more complex stories with simple vocabulary.

READING INDEPENDENTLY
Newly independent readers gain confidence reading more complex sentences with higher word counts.

READY TO READ MORE
Readers prepare for chapter books with fewer illustrations and longer paragraphs.

This book features sight words from the educator-supported Dolch Sight Words List. This encourages the reader to recognize commonly used vocabulary words, increasing reading speed and fluency.

For more information, please visit lbyr.com/passporttoreading.

Enjoy the journey!

Cover design by Ching N. Chan. Cover illustration by Maine Diaz.

Little, Brown and Company
Hachette Book Group
1290 Avenue of the Americas, New York, NY 10104
Visit us at LBYR.com

Originally published as *Spirit Riding Free: Lucky's Treasure Hunt*
in *Spirit Riding Free: Reading Adventures* by
Little, Brown and Company in August 2020
First Trade Paperback Edition: July 2021

Little, Brown and Company is a division of Hachette Book Group, Inc. The Little, Brown name and logo are trademarks of Hachette Book Group, Inc.

The publisher is not responsible for websites (or their content) that are not owned by the publisher.

Library of Congress Control Number: 2020946035

ISBNs: 978-0-316-49620-9 (pbk.), 978-0-316-49625-4 (ebook), 978-0-316-49621-6 (ebook), 978-0-316-49622-3 (ebook)

PRINTED IN CHINA

APS

10 9 8 7 6 5 4 3 2 1

Passport to Reading titles are leveled by independent reviewers applying the standards developed by Irene Fountas and Gay Su Pinnell in *Matching Books to Readers: Using Leveled Books in Guided Reading*, Heinemann, 1999.

DREAMWORKS
Spirit

LUCKY'S TREASURE HUNT

Adapted by Meredith Rusu

LITTLE, BROWN AND COMPANY

New York · Boston

Attention, Spirit fans!
Look for these words
when you read this book.
Can you spot them all?

cliff

treasure

skulls

crystals

Lucky is going camping with
her dad, Pru, and Abigail.

This is Lucky's first time camping.
She is excited!

Lucky wants to show her
dad that she is a brave
explorer just like he is.

Mr. Prescott leads the PALs
up a mountain trail.
It is dangerous!

He puts safety ropes
around the horses.

Spirit does not like wearing ropes.

He bumps into the wagon.

It falls over the cliff!

"It is okay," says Mr. Prescott.

"I will get the wagon tomorrow."

That night, the PALs
build a campfire.
Lucky's dad tells
the girls a story.

"I have this treasure map,"
Mr. Prescott says.

"It belonged to a man named Respero.
I never found the treasure."

"Maybe I will find it!" says Lucky.
She wants to go on adventures
like her dad does.

The next day, Mr. Prescott
leaves to get the wagon.

The girls look at
the treasure map.
It has a drawing on it.

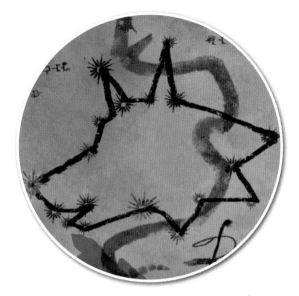

"It looks like a wolf!" Lucky says.

It is a clue.

"We should go to Wolf Ridge!"

Lucky and her friends
ride to Wolf Ridge.
They find another
clue there!

"Some of these rocks have symbols on them. The symbols are also on the map!" says Pru.

"I think we have to follow the rocks that match the map," Abigail says.

The girls reach the end of the path.

Big rocks crash down in front of them!

"That was close!" says Lucky.

"We should keep moving."

"It is getting late," says Abigail.
"Should we go back to camp?"

"Not yet," Lucky replies.
"We must be close to
finding the treasure!"

A cave is at the end of the path.
The PALs hurry inside it
and find a treasure chest.
It is locked!

There are pictures of skulls on the chest.
They look like the skulls on the map.
"I think I know how to open it!"
says Abigail.

She matches the skulls on the
chest to the ones on the map.
The chest unlocks!

Lucky takes a deep breath.

"This is it!" she says.

The PALs open the chest.

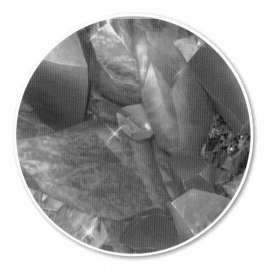

It is filled with beautiful crystals!

"Wow!" says Lucky.

"I cannot wait to show my dad!"

Suddenly, the PALs hear
a noise behind them.

It is a growl.

"A bear!" cries Lucky.

"Quick! We have to hide!"

Pru yells.

The PALs hide.

The bear is getting close.

A log crashes down.

It blocks the cave exit.

The girls are trapped!

Meanwhile, Lucky's dad
is looking for the PALs.

He sees Spirit running alone.
Where is Lucky?

Spirit leads Mr. Prescott to the cave.
They have to save the girls!

Spirit pulls a rope to move the log
that is blocking the cave exit.

The PALs escape just in time!

"We are sorry, Dad," says Lucky.

"We were following Respero's map."

"I am just glad
you are all right,"
Lucky's dad says.

The girls tell Mr. Prescott about how they found Respero's treasure.

They had such a fun adventure!

"You really are turning
into a brave explorer,"
Mr. Prescott tells Lucky.

"I guess it runs in the family,"
Lucky says.
She smiles.